Presented to

_____

From

_____

Date

_____

The PRESCHOOLERS
Family Story Book

The PRESCHOOLERS
Family Story Book

V. Gilbert Beers

with Kathleen Cathey, Janice Engel,
and Cynthia Grondahl

Illustrated by Teresa Walsh

VICTOR BOOKS

A DIVISION OF SCRIPTURE PRESS PUBLICATIONS INC.
USA CANADA ENGLAND

Published in Wheaton, Illinois by Victor Books/SP Publications, Inc.,
Wheaton, Illinois 60187

ISBN: 1-56476-492-3

Printed in the United States of America

2 3 4 5 6 7 Printing/Year 01 00 99 98 97 96

Contents

Something Wonderful Is about to Happen

Arlie and I have just embarked on our 15th preschool adventure—5 children and 10 grandchildren. The preschool years are special, you know, even more special than we often realize. It is during these wonderful years that the entire foundation for life is laid—physically, mentally, emotionally, spiritually. Most of our later life is shaped significantly during those vital years.These are truly the life- building years, perhaps even more than the college years.

Step by step, brick by brick, the qualities we call values are woven into your child's character during the preschool years. Values are simply Bible truths expressed as character traits. Kindness, generosity, honesty, truthfulness, and so on—these come from God's Word itself. But they need to be presented so that a preschool child can relate to them. That's what we have tried to do in *The Toddlers Bible, The Preschoolers Bible,* and now in this book. We want to make Bible learning fun and delightful, yet life-changing and vital.

At first, this book may look like a child's storybook—colorful, interesting, exciting, but still a child's storybook. You may even be tempted to think of it as ONLY a child's storybook. If you do, you and your child will miss something special. This is a carefully planned learning program, a program with strong life-building emphases, life building through the truths of God's Word.

The Preschoolers Family Story Book is designed to be used with *The Preschoolers Bible*. Be sure to look in the back of *The Preschoolers Bible* where you will find a comprehensive list of Bible doctrines, and another list of life-building values, your Preschooler will learn in that important Bible learning program. *The Preschoolers Family Story Book* helps your child learn many of those same Bible doctrines and life-building values.

As I first thought about this learning program, I thought of the 40+ years of joy and delight my wife Arlie and I had shared with our children and grandchildren. Then a wonderful idea leaped at me—why not develop this book with my three daughters? I have written more than 20 books with my son, but none with my daughters. This was the right one. When I approached them with the idea, they were enthusiastic.

Kathleen Cathey, that's right, Kathy Cathey, is a mother of three and participates with her husband Brad in their corporate graphics business. In addition, she teaches Kindermusik for preschool children at Wheaton College, Wheaton, Illinois. She has been an elementary public school teacher in music for three years, and for another three years taught music in a Mansio Mens Montessori preschool music program. She is a graduate of Wheaton College Conservatory of Music and studied cello for a year at the Mozarteum in Salzburg, Austria.

Janice Engel is a mother of three preschool children. She is a graduate of Wheaton College (Literature) where her husband Kevin now leads students in Christian outreach. Jan was Sunday School Coordinator at Hope Presbyterian Church in Richfield, Minnesota.

Cynthia Grondahl is a mother of one preschool child and is a graduate of Wheaton College (Christian Education). She recently put her husband Rob through Medical school by working as an executive secretary in a law firm. Cindy has been active in the Christian Education program at her local church.

As you might guess, the Christian life-building emphasis was basic in our home. We believed in fun and delight, but we believed that the life-changing truths of the Word should be woven into the fabric of mind and heart and character. Our four children and their mates share the passion that Arlie and I have to see preschoolers everywhere delight in God's Word and make it part of their own thought and being. Our prayer is that you and yours will also learn to delight in His truths, and that this book will help you along that road.

V. Gilbert Beers

SURPRISE!

"Surprise!" said Daddy. "We're going somewhere in the car. Please put your toys away."

"I don't want to put my toys away," said Alli. "I want to stay here and play."

"Me too," said Emily. "I don't want a ride in the car."

"But we have a special surprise for you," said Mommy. "It will be better than playing with your toys."

Alli and Emily kept playing with their toys. They even had a little pout on their faces. (Of course you would never have that, would you?)

"Now," said Daddy.

"OK," said Alli. But she didn't obey. She kept on playing with her toys. So did Emily.

"I'm going to get the car," said Daddy. "We leave in two minutes."

"So you have two minutes to pick up your toys," Mommy told the girls.

Now Alli and Emily picked up their toys. But they grumbled with every toy they picked up.

Alli and Emily grumbled as they got into the car.
They grumbled when they left the driveway. They
grumbled when Daddy parked the car downtown.
They kept on grumbling as they walked along the
street together.

"I wish I were home with my toys," said Alli.

"Me too," said Emily.

"Does anyone want to visit this furniture store?" Mommy asked. Alli and Emily looked quickly in the window.

"No!" they grumbled.

"How about this nice hardware store?" Daddy asked.

"Yuk!" said Alli.

"I want to go home," said Emily.

Alli and Emily didn't want to visit the shoe store
either. And they grumbled when they went by the
jewelry store.

"I want to play with my toys," said Alli.

"Me too," said Emily.

Mommy and Daddy smiled. Daddy even winked
at Mommy.

"How about this store?" Daddy asked. Alli and Emily began to grumble before they even looked. Then they stopped grumbling.

"Now what?" asked Mommy.

"Hamburger Hut!" Alli shouted.

"Yeah!" said Emily.

"Look who's here!" said Mommy.

"Grandpa!" shouted Alli.

"Grandma!" shouted Emily.

Alli and Emily ran inside as fast as they could go. Of course they had some big hugs for Grandma and Grandpa.

And, of course, Grandma and Grandpa had some big hugs for Alli and Emily.

"Well, I guess it's time to go home," said Daddy.

"That's right," said Mommy. "Alli and Emily want to play with their toys."

"NO!" shouted Alli. "We want to stay here with Grandpa and Grandma."

"Who wants to play with toys when we can do this?" said Emily.

"Is our surprise better than staying home with toys?" asked Mommy.

"MUCH better," said Alli.

"MUCH, MUCH better," said Emily.

"Let's remember that when God has special surprises for us," said Daddy.

Do you think they did?

Let's Talk!

Who has a special surprise for Alli and Emily?

What do Alli and Emily want to do instead?

What was the special surprise?

22

How did Alli and Emily like the surprise when they saw it?

What are some special surprises God has given you?

What should we do when God gives us a special surprise?

The Red Car

"That's my car," Jason shouted.

"No, it's my car," said Jon.

Mother frowned. "I haven't seen either of you play with that red car for weeks," she said. "Why is that one car so important now?"

"Because it's mine," said Jason.

"No, because it's mine," said Jon. Jason and Jon began to argue and fight. Mother couldn't hear all they said, but she did hear MINE, MINE, MINE, MINE at least ten times.

"Well, you won't get much playing done if you keep fighting," said Mother. "Let's do it this way. Jason can play with this red car for five minutes. Then Jon can play with it."

Jon grumbled as Jason began to play with the car. Jason drove it around Jon several times.

"See, it's really mine," said Jason.

"No, it's really mine," said Jon. "I'm just letting you have it for five minutes."

Then Mother heard MINE, MINE, MINE, and MINE at least ten more times.

"That idea didn't work," said Mother. "Let's try something different." Mother gave Jon a green car. She gave Jason a yellow car. Then she put the red MINE car on the shelf.

"Now have fun playing," she said.

Jason drove the yellow car around Jon. Jon drove the green car around Jason.

"But the red car is still mine," said Jason.

"No, it's mine," said Jon.

"This isn't working either," said Mother. "What can I do?"

Then Mother had another idea. "I'll play with the red car. Jason will play with the yellow car. Jon will play with the green car."

Jon and Jason both laughed a little when Mother got down on the floor. She made a noise like a car as she drove the red car around.

"Mother is certainly having fun with MY car,"
said Jason.

"She looks kind of funny playing with MY car,"
said Jon.

"MINE!" said Mother. But she felt strange calling
the car MINE.

Then Mother picked up the red car. She walked toward the door.

"Where are you going with MY car?" Jason asked.

"You're not taking MY car away, are you?" said Jon.

Mother smiled. "I'll be back soon," she said.

Jon and Jason were quiet while Mother was gone. Jon played with his green car. Jason played with his yellow car. Before long, Mother came back in the room. She had something in her hands. It was a package wrapped in gift wrap with a ribbon on it.

"What's that?" asked Jason.

"Where's MY red car?" asked Jon.

"This is JESUS' red car," said Mother. "I just gave it to Him. I even wrapped it up for Him."

Jon looked at Jason. Jason looked at Jon.

"I guess it's not my car anymore," said Jason.

"It's Jesus' car now," said Jon. "Do you think Jesus will let us play together with HIS car?" Mother smiled as she watched Jon and Jason play happily together with Jesus' car.

Let's Talk!

What did Jon and Jason both want?

Why do you think they both wanted the red car?

How did Mother try to help?

34

Mother gave the red car to someone special. Who was He?

How did this help Jon and Jason learn to play together?

Why do you think this pleased Jesus?

I'm Sorry

Katy didn't mean to break Mother's vase. She didn't want to break it. But she did break Mother's vase. Katy could see how sad Mother was. That made Katy sad too.

Katy knew she should say, "I'm sorry." Katy
wanted to say, "I'm sorry." But the words just would
not come out of Katy's mouth.

Mother wanted Katy to say, "I'm sorry." Mother knew that Katy wanted to say, "I'm sorry." But Mother knew that Katy could not say it. Mother could see the tears in Katy's eyes.

Katy ran to her room and Mother sat down to read a magazine. Before long Mother saw Katy come back with her doll. Mother pretended not to see her or hear her.

"I know you didn't want to break that vase," Katy said to her doll. "But you should tell me that you're sorry."

"I want to say 'I'm sorry,'" Katy made the doll say. "But the words just won't come out. It's so hard to say them."

"Let me help you," Katy said to her doll. Katy sat
for a long time. She said nothing. Then she began to
cry. "I'm sorry, I'm sorry, I'm sorry," she said. "Can
you say that with me, Dolly?"

"I'm sorry, I'm sorry, I'm sorry," the doll said.
Then Katy hugged her doll.

Katy put down her doll. She ran to Mother. "I'm sorry, I'm sorry, I'm sorry," Katy said to Mother.

Mother gave Katy the biggest hug she ever had. Katy gave Mother the biggest hug she ever had.

Do you think Katy was glad she said, "I'm sorry"?

Let's Talk!

What did Katy do that made Mother sad?

Why didn't Katy say, "I'm sorry"?

How did Katy's doll help her say, "I'm sorry"?

Did Katy ever tell
Mother, "I'm sorry"?

What did Mother do
then?

Is it ever hard for
you to say, "I'm sorry"?
How will this story help
you?

Ryan's Truck

"Tony and his family will be here for dinner tonight," Mother said to Ryan. "They have just come from another country. So Tony has no toys at all. Would you like to give him one of yours?"

Ryan looked around his room. He liked every one of his toys. He did not see one toy he wanted to give. "No," said Ryan. "I want to keep all of my toys."

Mother looked sad. "You have so many," she said. "Tony has none." Mother picked up the picture of Jesus on Ryan's dresser. "I wonder what Jesus would do for Tony?"

When Mother left, Ryan looked through his toys again. Then he saw an old game. Some of the pieces were lost and the box was beginning to fall apart. Ryan picked up the game. He took it to Mother. "I was going to throw this away," said Ryan. "I could give this to Tony."

Mother frowned. "Is that what you REALLY want to give Tony?" she asked.

Ryan took the beat-up old game back to his room.
He thought about the things Mother had said. He
would not want to get an old, beat-up game like that.
Tony would not want an old, beat-up game like that.
And Jesus would not give Tony an old, beat-up game
like that. Ryan put the game in the corner of his
room.

Ryan picked up a little car. He could give that to Tony. He wouldn't miss it. Then he thought of Tony getting the little car. Ryan was sad when he thought of Tony getting such a little gift. He wouldn't be pleased tonight when he gave the car to Tony. He was sure that Jesus would not be pleased tonight either.

Ryan looked at each of his toys. He thought of Tony when he looked at each one. He could see himself giving each one to Tony. He even thought he could see Jesus watching. "I wonder which toy Jesus would give Tony?" Ryan said to himself.

Suddenly Ryan knew what he wanted to do. He wanted to do what Jesus would do. Ryan picked up his favorite truck. He would give this to Tony.

That night Ryan gave Tony his special truck. Tony was almost the happiest boy in town. That's because Ryan was the happiest boy in town. Now he was sure that Jesus was happy too.

Let's Talk!

Why was it hard for Ryan to give something good to Tony?

Why did Ryan want to give the game and the little car at first?

Why didn't he give the game and the little car?

What did Ryan give Tony? Why did he do this?

Why was Tony happy? Why was Ryan happier?

Do you like to give? Why do you think giving pleases Jesus?

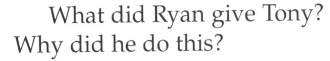

What Do You Want
for Your Birthday?

"What do you want for your birthday?" Grandpa asked Kevin.

"A boom box, a high-flying electronic Distendo, Super Electric Sneakers, a TV for my room, and a puppy," said Kevin.

Grandpa chuckled. "If you get too much, you won't think any of it is special," he said. Kevin thought for a long time about that. He thought about playing with all those things. Perhaps Grandpa was right!

"What do you want for your birthday?" Grandma asked Kevin.

"A high-flying electronic Distendo, Super Electric Sneakers, a TV for my room, and a puppy," said Kevin.

Grandma chuckled. "If you get too much, you won't think any of it is special," she said. Kevin thought for a long time about that. He thought about playing with all those things. Perhaps Grandpa and Grandma were right!

"What do you want for your birthday?" Kevin's big brother asked him.

"Super Electric Sneakers, a TV for my room, and a puppy," said Kevin.

Big brother chuckled. "If you get too much, you won't think any of it is special," he said. Kevin thought for a long time about that. He thought about playing with all those things. Perhaps Grandpa and Grandma and big brother were right!

"What do you want for your birthday?" Mother asked Kevin.

"A TV for my room and a puppy," said Kevin.

"If you get both of those, you won't think either is special," said Mother. Kevin thought for a long time about that. He thought about watching TV and trying to play with a puppy. Perhaps Grandpa, Grandma, big brother, and Mother were right!

"What do you want for your birthday?" Father
asked Kevin.

"A puppy," said Kevin.

Father chuckled. "Happy birthday," he said. Now Kevin was happy that he really and truly had not asked for too much. This would be the very best birthday ever, playing with his puppy.

Let's Talk!

What did Kevin tell each person that he wanted for his birthday?

How did each person help him change his mind?

Is it bad to get too much? Why?

Do you ever want too much for your birthday or Christmas?

What did you learn from this story about asking for too much?

Do you remember to thank Jesus for what you DO have? Will you now?

Who Spilled Milk in My Chair?

"Who spilled milk in my chair?" Mother asked. Luke looked at Amy. Amy looked at Luke.

They had been careless with a glass of milk. They had spilled it in Mother's chair.

"I didn't do it," said Luke.

"I didn't do it," said Amy. Luke and Amy were sure no one had seen them do it.

"Perhaps Kitty spilled the milk," said Amy.

"Kitty was in the kitchen with me," said Mother.

"I know that Kitty did not do it."

"Perhaps Puppy spilled it," said Luke.

"Puppy was in the kitchen with me too," said
Mother. "I know that Puppy did not do it."

Mother said nothing more. She got some sponges and cleaned her chair. Amy and Luke watched as she did this. But they said nothing more either. They were sure no one had seen them spill the milk.

"Did either of you see who spilled the milk?"
Mother asked.

"No, I didn't see it," said Amy.

"I didn't either," said Luke.

"I suppose no one saw what happened," said
Amy.

"So we will never know who spilled the milk,"
said Luke.

"But Someone did see who spilled the milk," said
Mother. "He's in this house right now!"

Amy looked surprised. Luke looked surprised
too. "Someone saw who spilled the milk?" Amy
asked. "Did you?"

"No, I didn't see who spilled the milk," said Mother. "But Jesus did. He knows what happened. He's here with us now." Amy looked at Luke. Luke looked at Amy. Amy could see some tears in Luke's eyes. Luke could see some tears in Amy's eyes.

"Does Jesus REALLY know who spilled the milk?" Amy asked.

"Did He REALLY see us?" asked Luke.

"Yes," said Mother. "He really did see you. And He really does know exactly who spilled the milk."

"I'm sorry," said Amy. "Luke and I both spilled the milk. Please forgive me."

"I'm sorry too," said Luke. "We didn't mean to spill it. And I'm sorry we didn't tell you the truth. Please forgive me." Amy and Luke both gave Mother the biggest hug ever. And Mother gave them the biggest hug ever too.

"I forgive you," she said.

Isn't that what you do when you love someone very much?

Let's Talk!

Who really did spill the milk in Mother's chair?

Why didn't Amy and Luke tell her that they spilled the milk?

Who saw Amy and Luke spill the milk?

Who sees everything YOU do?

Did Amy and Luke ever tell Mother who spilled the milk? Why?

What did Mother do then?

Moms

Some moms have funny noses.

And some have lots of curls.

Some have a son who weighs a ton.

Some have 200 girls!

Some moms can fly.

And some can jump.

And some sleep in a tree.

But of all the moms

In all the world

YOU'RE THE BEST FOR ME!

Let's Talk!

What kind of moms did you meet here?

How were these moms different?

Who made all these moms different?

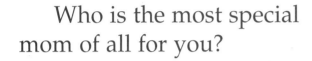

Who is the most special mom of all for you?

What makes your mom special?

Have you thanked your mom today for the things she does?

Dear God, What Can I Give You?

Dear God, I want to give You a special gift.
But I don't know what You want.
Will You please help me?

I thought about giving You a basketball.

But Father said no one would play on the OTHER team.

He said You could make swish shots a hundred miles away.

Wow! You must REALLY be good.

I saw some special sneakers in the store today.
But my big brother said You don't need to run.
He said You're everywhere at the same time.
How do You DO that, God?

One store had a wonderful builder's set.

But Grandpa said You can build anything, even without a set.

He said You even made the whole world.

You didn't even have a builder's set!

I thought I had just the gift for You.

It's a BIG red apple, like the one I gave my teacher.

But my teacher said You made the apple tree.

I guess You can have all the apples You want.

I asked Grandma if You would like a puppy for a present.

She smiled and said You made all the puppies in the world.

You really have a lot of puppies, don't You!

Is that why You want us kids to help You feed them?

My Sunday School teacher said You don't need a
shirt or tie.

She didn't think You wear those things.

I wish I didn't have to wear those things either!

Anyway, I guess I don't know what size You wear.

Mom says, "Don't try to buy anything for God.
He can make anything He wants."
Could You teach ME how to do that?

Mom says there is one special gift You want.
Then she told me what it is.

"God wants you to love Him and talk with Him," she said.

"He wants you to learn about Him from His special Book, the Bible."

Dear God, is that what You really want
More than anything else?
I can't wrap that gift up for You,
But I will try to give it to You every day.

Let's Talk!

What special gifts did this boy think about giving to God?

Why didn't he give each one?

What are some things that God made?

Why can't you make the things God made?

What gift did the boy really want to give to God?

Can you give this gift to God? Will you?

Thank You, God, for Sunshine

Thank You, God, for sunshine.
How did You make something so wonderful?
How did You make sunshine in so many wonderful ways?

Thank You, God, for "Good Morning" sunshine.
Sunrise chases the night away.
Good morning sunshine gives me a brand new
day.

Thank You, God, for "Playtime" sunshine.
Playtime sunshine helps me splash in my back-
yard pool. It smiles while I have a picnic with my
family.

Thank You, God, for "Hide-and-go-seek" sunshine. Do you see the puffy white clouds in the sky? They are playing "hide-and-go-seek" with the sunshine.

Thank You, God, for "Time-to-grow" sunshine.

This morning I planted some seeds. The rain gave them a drink of water. Then the sunshine smiled and said, "Time to grow!"

Thank You, God, for "Keep-me-warm" sunshine.
When Your sunshine is hiding I have to wear a
coat to keep warm.
But I'm not wearing my coat now! I'm hot!

Thank You, God, for "Turn-on-the-light" sunshine.

Sometimes it's so dark and scary at night. Then You send Your sunshine.

It's like someone turning on a BIG light in the sky.

Thank You, God, for "Make-me-a-shadow" sunshine.

I have so much fun with my shadow. How could I
do that without Your wonderful sunshine?

Thank You, God, for "Good-night" sunshine.
Sunset is a soft, pretty time. It says,
"Sleepytime is coming soon."

Thank You, God, for all kinds of sunshine.

You made our wonderful world bright and beautiful.

You do wonderful things because You're such a special person.

I guess that's why I love You so much!

Let's Talk!

Who gives us sunshine?

What are some special things sunshine does for us?

What would happen if the sun stopped shining?

What are some things you like to do on a sunny day?

Are you glad God made sunshine?

Have you thanked God today for sunshine? Will you?

Doesn't God Like Elephants?

A trip to the zoo was always fun. Sarah thought it was even more fun to visit the zoo with Father. Father thought it was fun to go with Sarah too!

First they went to see the elephants.

"Doesn't God like elephants?" Sarah asked.
Father looked puzzled. "Why?" he asked.
"Because He gave elephants such funny noses," said Sarah. "I'm glad He didn't give me a nose like that."

"God gave you hands and fingers," said Father. "You can pick up things easily. But elephants don't have hands and fingers. They need their funny noses to pick up things."

"Doesn't God like giraffes?" Sarah asked.
Father looked puzzled. "Why?" he asked.
"Because He gave giraffes such funny long
necks," said Sarah. "I'm glad He didn't give me a
neck like that."

"God gave you hands and fingers," said Father. "You can reach up into a tree and pick things. But giraffes don't have hands and fingers. They need long necks so they can reach up into a tree or far away to get their food."

"Doesn't God like zebras?" Sarah asked.
Father looked puzzled. "Why?" he asked.
"Because He gave zebras such funny swishy tails,
like horses' tails," said Sarah. "I'm glad He didn't
give me a swishy tail like that."

"God gave you hands and fingers," said Father. "If flies bother you, you can shoo them away. But zebras and horses and cows don't have hands and fingers. They need their swishy tails to shoo flies away."

"Doesn't God like chickens and ducks and geese?" Sarah asked.

Father looked puzzled. "Why?" he asked.

"Because He gave them such funny bills," said Sarah. "I'm glad He didn't give me a funny bill like that."

"God gave you hands and fingers," said Father. "You can pick up your food with forks and spoons in your hands. But chickens and ducks and geese need their bills to pick up their food."

Sarah thought for a long time. "I'm glad I don't have an elephant's nose, a giraffe's neck, a swishy tail, and a funny bill," she said. "Thank You, God, for fingers and hands. You really did know what You were doing, didn't You?"

Let's Talk!

Where did Sarah and her father see all these animals?

How was Sarah different from the animals she saw?

What did Sarah have that none of these animals had?

What can you do with your hands and fingers?

Pretend that you have no hands and fingers. How would you touch?

Have you thanked God for your hands and fingers? Will you now?

I Can't Do It

"I can't do it," Brian whimpered. Brian wanted to put a wooden puzzle together. But the puzzle didn't go together the way he thought it should. "I just can't do it," he whimpered again.

"Let me watch how you do it," said Father. "Perhaps I can help." So Brian picked up a piece of the wooden puzzle. It fit in the right place. But the second piece did not fit where he thought it should go.

"See," he said. "I can't do it." Brian even kicked his feet in a little bit of anger.

"Try it again," said Father. "I think I see the problem." Brian picked up the first piece of the puzzle. It was easy. It fit in the right place. But the second piece did not fit where Brian thought it should go.

"See," said Brian. "I told you that I can't do it."

"I see what's wrong," said Father. "You can do it, but the puzzle can't do it." Brian looked surprised. "What do you mean?" Brian asked.

"Let me show you," said Father. He picked up the first piece of the puzzle. He put it in the same place that Brian had put it. "That one is easy," said Father. "Now let's put the second piece where you put it." Father picked up the second piece of the puzzle. He put it in the same place that Brian had put it. Of course it did not fit.

"That's not the right place for that piece," said Brian.

"I know," said Father. "But that piece is stubborn. It just won't go where it should. OK, puzzle, make that piece go where it should." Father did not even touch the piece of the puzzle. "Go on," Father said to the piece of the puzzle. "Go where you should."

Brian laughed. "The piece of the puzzle won't go by itself," he said. "We have to move it to other places until it fits."

"Really?" said Father. "Would you like to show me?" Brian moved the piece of the puzzle here. He moved it there. Suddenly it fit in just the right place.

"Do you think the third piece would fit that easily?" Father asked.

"Of course," said Brian. "Watch." Brian picked up the third piece. He moved it here. He moved it there. He kept moving it until it fit where it should.

Father smiled. "I think Brian learned something important from this puzzle," he said.

"I think so too," said Brian. "I learned that puzzle pieces won't put themselves in the right places. I learned that I have to keep trying until something works."

"Thank You, God, for helping Brian learn something very important," Father whispered. Did you learn something important too?

Let's Talk!

What did Brian say he couldn't do?

How did Father help him put the puzzle together?

What do you think Brian learned when Father helped him?

Have you learned something special from Father or Mother today?

Have you thanked them?

Will you thank them now?

I'm Too Tired

"Time to put your toys away," said Mother. "We need to wash and get ready for bed." Christopher looked at all the toys he had scattered over the floor. He was sure he had every one of his toys there.

"I'm too tired," he moaned.

Mother frowned. "I'm too tired, too," she said. "So who should pick up your toys?"

Christopher looked at Mother. He could see she was tired. She had worked hard all day. He really didn't want Mother to have to pick them up. And he didn't know what to say. If he didn't pick up his toys and Mother didn't pick them up, who would?

"But I'm too tired," said Christopher.

"So I'll have to pick them up," said Mother. "But if I do, I'll put them all in my room. You might not get to play with them tomorrow."

"Why can't we just leave all the toys on the floor tonight?" said Christopher. Mother frowned again.

"You won't mind if someone steps on them and breaks some of them tonight? OK, we can leave them there if that makes you happy."

Christopher put on his PJs. He brushed his teeth and scrubbed his face. Mother helped him, of course. But he forgot about the toys and ran into his room. Guess what happened. Christopher tripped over some of his toys and fell down. He even broke one of his favorite cars.

Christopher sat down on the floor. He looked at the toys. He was too tired to pick them up. But he didn't want Mother to put them away in her room. And he didn't want to break any more of his favorite toys.

"I have an idea," said Christopher. "If I pick up my toys would you like to help me?" Mother smiled.

"I was waiting for you to ask," she said. "Let's play a picking-up game. Before we wink an eye, we'll have them all picked up."

Mother and Christopher sang some songs as they picked up toys.

They even played a game about picking up.

Before long all the toys were picked up. "That was fun," said Christopher. "Can we do that tomorrow night too?"

Mother smiled. "I'm sure we can. But now it's time to pray. You're not too tired to do that, are you?"

Let's Talk!

What did Mother want Christopher to do?

Why didn't he want to pick up his toys?

How did Christopher break one of his cars?

Who picked up the toys?

How did Christopher and his Mother have fun picking up the toys?

What was the last thing Christopher did that day? Why?

The Jesus Gift Box

"Thank you for helping me feed kitty, Melissa," said Mother. "Now we can put that in our JESUS GIFT BOX." Mother wrote, "Melissa helped feed kitty," and put the slip of paper into the shoe box. Mother had printed JESUS GIFT BOX on the top.

"Thank you for helping me set the table, Myron," said Mother. "Now we can put that in our JESUS GIFT BOX." Mother wrote, "Myron helped set the table," and put the slip of paper into the shoe box.

Later that day Melissa helped Mother dry some dishes. Mother wrote that on a little slip of paper and put it into the JESUS GIFT BOX.

"When can we open the JESUS GIFT BOX?"
asked Melissa.

"On Sunday, after church and Sunday dinner,"
said Father.

On Tuesday Father put a slip into the box. It said, "Myron helped sweep the garage."

On Thursday Mother put another slip into the box. It said, "Melissa helped clean her room."

On Saturday Mother and Father put slips into the box. They had helped each other with some chores. They laughed when they came to the box at the same time.

On Sunday Melissa and Myron could hardly wait to open the JESUS GIFT BOX. When everyone had finished eating dinner, Father brought the JESUS GIFT BOX to the table. Slowly he lifted the lid. Then Father prayed, "Dear Jesus, we did all these special things because we love each other. But we also did them because we love You. Now we want to give these gifts to You today."

Father took a slip from the box. "Myron helped set the table," he read. "That was your gift to Mother, Myron," said Father. "Do you also want to give that gift to Jesus?" Myron smiled.

"Yes," he said. Father read another slip.

"Melissa helped feed kitty."

"I want to give that gift to Jesus too," said Melissa.

At last all the slips of paper had been read. Father and Mother, Melissa and Myron had given each of their family gifts to Jesus. "Now we can start over, can't we?" said Melissa.

"Yes," said Father. "You can give brand new gifts to each other and to Jesus."

Would you like to give some special gifts to your family and to Jesus this week?

Let's Talk!

What did Mother or Father put into the JESUS GIFT BOX?

When did the family open the box?

What did Father pray before they opened the box?

Do you like to do special things for family members? Why?

Do you like to do special things for Jesus?

Would you like to make a JESUS GIFT BOX?

The BIG, BIG Box

"It's just a washing machine box." That's what the man said when he left it for Jory and Joshua. But Jory and Joshua never believed that for a moment. The BIG, BIG box was MUCH, MUCH more than just a washing machine box.

On Monday the BIG, BIG box became a castle. Of course every castle must have a king and a queen. You may think the king and queen look like Jory and Joshua. You may think the castle may even look a little like a washing machine box. But to Jory and Joshua, this is the finest castle and the most handsome king and queen ever. You may think so too!

On Tuesday, the BIG, BIG box became a spaceship. Jory wanted to fly it first. So Joshua acted like a gentleman and let her. Hold on! This spaceship is going out to the farthest stars. Would you like to go with them? You can, you know.

On Wednesday, the BIG, BIG box became a secret clubhouse. Jory and Joshua would only let special people inside. Would you like to go in? Just say your name. That's the special code word. Ready?

On Thursday, the BIG, BIG box became a filling station. Would you like to pull your car up in front? You may, you know. This is a very special filling station. The people in charge will help you get your gas and clean your car windows.

On Friday, the BIG, BIG box became our house.
"Time to get dinner!" someone says.

"Time to set the table," someone else says.

"Time to brush your teeth," says another. Does
this sound like your house? It could be, you know.

On Saturday, the BIG, BIG box became our van. "Hurry and get the children," someone says. "We have to go grocery shopping." Guess who will drive today? Would you like to go along? You can, you know.

On Sunday, the BIG, BIG box became our Sunday School. "Be sure to bring your Bible," someone says.

"Which song would you like to sing this morning?" someone else asks. What else do you do in your Sunday School?

Would you like to visit Jory and Joshua this afternoon? Would you like to play with them in their BIG, BIG box? What would you like for it to become now?

Thank You, dear God, that I can play each day.
Thank You for helping me have so much fun, even
with a BIG, BIG box.

Let's Talk!

What kind of box was the BIG, BIG box at first?

What did it become?

What other things would you like the box to become?

Do you like to play?

Play is a special gift from God. Have you thanked Him for it?

Would you like to thank God now that you can play?

Three Grains of Corn

Once, long ago, there was a wise old mouse who lived with some other mice in an old barn. The wise old mouse was always helping the younger mice learn important lessons. So one day he called three younger mice, Fred, Ed, and Jed, to see him.

"I have three grains of corn," he said. "I will give each of you one grain of corn. Come back in a week and tell me how you have used this grain of corn wisely."

Fred bowed and said, "Thank you" and took his grain of corn back to his hiding place.

Ed bowed and said, "Thank you" and took his grain of corn back to his hiding place.

Jed bowed and said, "Thank you" and took his grain of corn back to his hiding place.

The wise old mouse went to his hiding place and took a long nap.

Fred looked at his grain of corn. It looked so good and he felt so hungry. "I think eating is a very wise way to use this corn," said Fred. "It will help me grow. It will keep me from being hungry. And it will not be there for someone to steal." So Fred sat down to a wonderful meal. Before long, his grain of corn was gone.

Ed looked at his grain of corn. He thought about eating it too. He thought about many things he could do with the grain of corn. But he couldn't decide which one to do. So Ed put his grain of corn in a box. Then he hid the box in a dark corner.

Jed looked at his grain of corn. He too thought
about eating it. But he knew it would be gone. He
thought about many things he could do with the
grain of corn. Then he decided that he would plant it.
Jed dug the ground and made it soft. He planted the
grain of corn and put water on it. Then he waited for
it to grow.

At the end of the week, Fred, Ed, and Jed went to see the wise old mouse. "Well," said the wise old mouse. "What did you do with the grains of corn I gave you?"

"I ate mine," said Fred. "It was good."

"I'm glad you enjoyed it," said the wise old mouse. "Your grain of corn has served you, but now it is gone."

"I hid mine," said Ed. "I just can't decide what to do with it."

The wise old mouse smiled. "You have gained nothing and you have lost nothing," he said.

"I planted mine," said Jed. "It will grow and give me a big ear of corn with many grains. Then I will give one grain back to you. I will plant another grain. And I will still have corn to eat for a long time."

"You are the wisest of all," said the wise old mouse. Why do you think the wise old mouse is right?

Let's Talk!

What did the wise old mouse give the other three? Why?

What did each of the three young mice do with his grain of corn?

Why do you think Fred ate his corn?

Why do you think Ed hid his corn?

Why do you think Jed planted his corn?

Which young mouse was wisest of all? Why?

Two Pencils

Taylor looked so sad when Mother picked him up at Tim's house. "You look so sad," said Mother. "Is something the matter?"

Taylor frowned. "I'm sad because Tim makes his letters so much better than mine," said Taylor. "It's not fair."

"Why do you think his letters are better?" Mother asked.

"Because he has a prettier pencil," said Taylor. "If my pencil was better than his, I could make better letters than his." Now Mother frowned.

"Let's try that when we get home," she said.

Mother looked around the house for some pencils. She found an old, beat-up pencil that looked as if it should be thrown away. Then she found a pretty pencil. Taylor thought it was even nicer than Tim's pencil.

"Let me see what I can do with these two pencils," said Mother. She picked up the pretty pencil and wrote T A Y L O R. But the letters were squiggly and did not look good at all.

Taylor laughed. "You can do better than that," he said. "I know you can."

Mother picked up the old, beat-up pencil. She wrote T A Y L O R. This time the letters were beautiful. They looked so nice. Taylor looked surprised.

Taylor picked up the pretty pencil. He looked at it carefully. Then he picked up the old pencil. He looked at it carefully. "How did you do that?" he asked. "You made that old pencil write better than the pretty pencil."

"It's not the pencil," said Mother. "It's the way we use the pencil. Now you try it." Taylor wrote T A Y L O R first with the pretty pencil. Then he wrote T A Y L O R with the old pencil.

"Well?" said Mother.

Taylor held both pencils up and looked at them.
"I think I wrote better with the old pencil," he said.
"I think you did too," said Mother.

"God can do wonderful things through us, just like we wrote wonderful things with the old pencil," said Mother. "It doesn't matter if we are pretty or not so pretty. It doesn't matter if we're big or little, tall or short."

"I'm glad," said Taylor. "Thank You, God." Are you glad God can do special things through you, no matter how pretty or handsome you are?

Let's Talk!

Why was Taylor sad when Mother picked him up?

What did Taylor think a pretty pencil could do?

What did Mother do with the two pencils?

Does a better-looking pencil REALLY write better? Why not?

Can God do wonderful things through people who are not so pretty or handsome?

Does God want to do wonderful things through you and me? Let's let Him!

The Biggest Gift of All

Randy's birthday party was almost over. His friends had brought him some wonderful gifts. Now Randy's mother had a surprise for the birthday guests. "I have five gifts here," she said. "There is one for each of you."

Before Randy's mother could say another word,
Randy's little brother Byron rushed up and put his
hands on the biggest gift. "I want that one," he said.

"You'll have to wait," said Randy's mother. "We haven't decided how to give these gifts. When we decide that, you will know which gift you will get."

But that wasn't good enough for Byron. He was sure that the biggest gift must be the best gift. Byron wanted the best gift. He didn't care what the others got. So Byron put on a tantrum. "I want that gift," he shouted.

Randy was embarrassed by his little brother. The other friends were embarrassed by Byron too. "Oh, let him have it," someone said.

So Randy's mother asked all the other friends, "Shall we let Byron have the biggest gift?" They all said yes. They were glad to do anything to make Byron quiet.

"You may have this gift, but you MUST not open it until everyone opens their gifts," said Randy's mother. "Also, you MUST understand that the biggest gift isn't always the best gift." Byron nodded his head yes. Then he sat down and clutched the biggest gift. He was sure that biggest WAS best.

Randy's mother wrote numbers on slips of paper. Each of Randy's friends chose a number. The friend with number 1 opened his gift first. It was a cute, cuddly stuffed puppy. The person with number 2 opened his gift. It was exactly the same cute, cuddly stuffed puppy. So were number 3 and number 4.

At last it was time for Byron to open his gift. He liked the cuddly puppies the others had received. He was sure his gift was something MUCH better. But when Byron opened the big box, he found the same cute, cuddly stuffed puppy inside. "But...but...," he started to say.

"I just happened to have a bigger box for that one," said Randy's mother. "But Byron, I think you learned an important lesson today. Bigger is not always better."

Byron looked sad. Then he began to laugh. Then all of Randy's friends thought that was a great lesson to learn too. "That really is a good lesson to learn," another boy said. "I will remember it for a long, long time." Do you think any of Randy's friends ever forgot that bigger is not always better? Will you?

Let's Talk!

Who wanted the biggest-looking gift? Why?

Why was it wrong for Byron to want the biggest gift?

What did each of Randy's friends get from his mother?

What was in the BIG gift that Byron had?

What did you learn from this story?

Why doesn't Jesus want us to be greedy like Byron?

The Swimming Pool

"Susan is my very best friend," Samantha told her father. Father looked surprised.

"Not long ago you said you didn't like Susan," he said. "What happened?"

"I didn't like her," said Samantha. "She was bossy and rude to me." Father smiled.

"So now she isn't bossy and rude to you?"

"Yes, she still is," said Samantha.

"Let's talk about this some more," said Father. "Susan is bossy and rude, but you still like to play with her. She's even your very best friend."

"But I don't like to play with her," said Samantha.

"Wait, wait, wait," said Father. "I need help. Susan is bossy and rude to you. You don't even like to play with her. But she's your best friend? What do you mean by 'best friend,' Samantha?"

"Well, I like to go to her house after school," said Samantha. "So doesn't that make her my best friend?"

"Why do you like to go to her house?" asked Father.

"Because I like to swim in her pool," said Samantha.

Father smiled. "Now I understand," he said. "Susan isn't really your best friend. Susan's pool is your best friend. Is that what you're saying?"

Samantha thought for a long time. "I ... I guess Susan can't really be my best friend as long as she is bossy and rude to me," she said. "I ... I guess I just go there because I like her pool."

"Do you really want your best friend to be a swimming pool?" asked Father. "Or would you rather have a really good friend as your best friend?"

"I want my best friend to be a really good friend," said Samantha. "Why don't we ask Jesus to help me find the kind of friend He wants me to have." So Samantha and Father prayed together. They asked Jesus to help Samantha find a truly very best friend. Have you asked Jesus to help you do that too?

Let's Talk!

Why did Samantha like to go to Susan's house?

What kind of person was Susan?

Do you like friends who are bossy and rude? Why not?

Do your friends want you to be bossy or rude? Why not?

Father and Samantha asked Someone to help her find a new friend. Who was He?

How can Jesus help us find good friends?

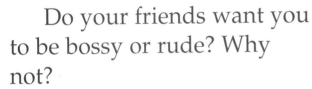

Tammy's Kindness

Tammy saw the neighbor lady next door mowing her lawn. She was working so hard and looked so hot. Then Tammy had a good idea. "Mother, may I take Mrs. Duckworth a glass of lemonade?" Mother smiled.

"That would be wonderful," she said. "Let me help you."

"What a sweet girl," said Mrs. Duckworth when Tammy gave her the lemonade. "Thank you for being so kind. Why are you doing this for me?"

Tammy smiled. "I'm doing it for you AND Jesus," she said. "I think Jesus wants us to be kind to one another."

Mrs. Duckworth was still thinking about Tammy's lemonade when she saw the mailman coming down the street. "I have an idea," she thought. "Tammy was kind to me. Why don't I do something special for the mailman?"

"What a kind lady," the mailman said when Mrs. Duckworth gave him a drink of cold water. "Thank you for being so kind. Why are you doing this for me?"

Mrs. Duckworth smiled. "I'm doing it for you AND Jesus," she said. "I think Jesus wants us to be kind to one another."

The mailman was still thinking about Mrs. Duckworth's cold water when he saw a lady coming down the street with a big bag of groceries. "I have an idea," he thought. "Mrs. Duckworth was kind to me. Why don't I help that lady with her groceries?"

"What a kind gentleman," Mrs. Walsh said when the mailman carried her groceries to her house. "Thank you for being so kind. Why are you doing this for me?"

The mailman smiled. "I'm doing it for you AND Jesus," he said. "I think Jesus wants us to be kind to one another."

Mrs. Walsh was still thinking about that when she saw Mr. Watkins sitting on his porch. "He probably hasn't had a good lunch for a long time," she thought. So Mrs. Walsh made a lovely lunch and took it to Mr. Watkins.

"What a kind person you are," said Mr. Watkins. "Thank you for being so kind. Why are you doing this for me?"

Mrs. Walsh smiled. "I'm doing it for you AND Jesus," she said. "I think Jesus wants us to be kind to one another."

Mr. Watkins was still thinking about that when he saw Tammy playing across the street. "I have an idea," he thought. "Mrs. Walsh was so kind to me. Why don't I do something special for my neighbor girl?" Mr. Watkins saw the ice cream truck coming as he rang the doorbell at Tammy's house.

"May I buy Tammy an ice cream bar?" Mr. Watkins asked Tammy's mother.

"What a kind person you are," said Tammy's mother. "Wouldn't it be nice if more people were so kind? Yes, you may do that for Tammy."

"Thank you for being so kind," Tammy said to Mr. Watkins. "But why are you doing this for me?"

Mr. Watkins smiled. "I'm doing it for you AND Jesus," he said. "I think Jesus wants us to be kind to one another." Tammy smiled. She almost thought she had heard that somewhere before. Do you think she had?

Let's Talk!

What did Tammy do for Mrs. Duckworth?

What other kind things came from Tammy's kind thing?

Why did each person do something kind?

How did Tammy's kindness come back to her?

Does Jesus like for you to be kind to others? Why?

What kindness can you do today? Will you?

If I Could Make the World

If I could help God
Make the world,
I'll tell you
What I'd do.

I'd make the sky
Look purple,
And all the grass
Look blue.

I'd make the clouds
With stripes and dots,
And add some
Circles too.

242

I'd make the cows
Fly in the sky;
I'd make the birds
Go MOO.

Each dog and cat
Would wear a hat,
And walk
Like people do.

244

And all the
Jungle animals
Would have
A people zoo.

Each tree would have
A hand or foot,
And maybe wear
A shoe.

I'd give us each
A dozen eyes,
Instead of
Only two.

But I suppose
It's better,
For God alone
To do,

The stuff
That God does best,
For me,
And for YOU.

Let's Talk!

What would this person do to change God's world?

Do you like any of the things he would do? Why not?

Who made our wonderful world?

Do you think God did a good job?

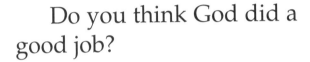

Are you glad for the way He made it?

Will you tell Him so today? Will you thank Him now?

251